The Super-Smelly Moldy Blob

Read more Olive & Beatrix books!

Olive & Beatrix

The Super-Smelly Moldy Blob

by Amy Marie Stadelmann

BRANCHES

SCHOLASTIC INC.

For Mom and Scott, because
"No one messes with library books!"

Copyright © 2015 by Amy Marie Stadelmann

All rights reserved. Published by Scholastic Inc. *Publishers since 1920.*
SCHOLASTIC, BRANCHES, and associated logos are trademarks and/or registered trademarks of Scholastic Inc.

The publisher does not have any control over and does not assume any responsibility for author or third-party websites and their content.

No part of this publication may be reproduced, stored in a retrieval system, or transmitted in any form or by any means, electronic, mechanical, photocopying, recording, or otherwise, without written permission of the publisher. For information regarding permission, write to Scholastic Inc., Attention: Permissions Department, 557 Broadway, New York, NY 10012.

This book is a work of fiction. Names, characters, places, and incidents are either the product of the author's imagination or are used fictitiously, and any resemblance to actual persons, living or dead, business establishments, events, or locales is entirely coincidental.

Library of Congress Cataloging-in-Publication Data

Stadelmann, Amy Marie, author, illustrator.
The Super-Smelly Moldy Blob / by Amy Marie Stadelmann. — First edition.
pages cm. — (Olive & Beatrix ; 2)
Summary: Beatrix wins the school science fair every year because she uses magic to cheat, but this year her un-magical twin Olive is convinced that her own project on molds will win—until a fight over space upsets both projects and turns Olive's mold into a stinky, moldy blob monster which is alive, growing, and threatening to overwhelm the school.

ISBN 0-545-81484-7 (pbk. : alk. paper) — ISBN 0-545-81485-5 (hardcover : alk. paper) — ISBN 0-545-81486-3 (ebook) — ISBN 0-545-81487-1 (eba ebook) 1. Witches—Juvenile fiction. 2. Twins—Juvenile fiction. 3. Sisters—Juvenile fiction. 4. Science projects—Juvenile fiction. 5. Magic—Juvenile fiction. 6. Competition (Psychology)—Juvenile fiction. [1. Witches—Fiction. 2. Twins—Fiction. 3. Sisters—Fiction. 4. Science projects—Fiction. 5. Schools—Fiction. 6. Magic—Fiction. 7. Competition (Psychology)—Fiction.]
I. Title.
PZ7.1.S72Su 2015
[Fic]—dc23
2015011355

ISBN 978-0-545-81485-0 (hardcover) / ISBN 978-0-545-81484-3 (paperback)

10 9 8 7 6 5 4 3 2 1   15 16 17 18 19/0

Printed in China   38
First edition, October 2015
Edited by Katie Carella
Book design by Becky James

Table of Contents

The Science Un-Fair

Hi, my name is Olive. And this is my twin sister, Beatrix. Even though we are twins, we're nothing alike!

Beatrix may look like an ordinary girl, but she's not. She is a witch.

Knows how to cast magic spells

Talking pet pig

Gets around by flying on a broomstick

The name is Houston. And I am no one's <u>pet</u>.

I may also look like an ordinary girl. That's because I am. I'm not a witch at all.

Knows how to spell <u>Mississippi</u>

Pile of books

Gets around by walking (and sometimes skipping)

What's that smell?

Holy Moldy!

SCIENCE

Beatrix has always used her magic powers to get things done.

I think this makes her kind of lazy.

I have always had to use my good old-fashioned brainpower to get things done.

I think this makes me pretty smart.

We live in the quiet town of Juniper Hollows. Our house is just down the road from Juniper Hollows Elementary School.

JUNIPER
HOLLOWS
ELEMENTARY
SCHOOL

school

our house

Eddie's house

My best friend, Eddie, lives next door.

Eddie

Eddie and I create fantastic and mind-blowing science projects.

Every year, our school holds a Science Fair. And every year, Eddie and I each try to win the blue ribbon.

But my sister always wins. It's not fair because Beatrix's science experiments are not even <u>scientific</u> . . .

Oh, and did I mention that Eddie loves making up songs?

This year, the fair is going to be different. Eddie and I have worked extra hard on our projects.

May the Best Twin Win

On Saturday morning, Beatrix and I left bright and early—before all the other students.

I wanted to get the best spot at the fair. And so did Beatrix.

We rushed into the gym. It was all set up. There were rows of tables waiting to be filled with projects.

The best table <u>by far</u> was the one way up front by the judges' table. Beatrix and I both had our eyes on it.

the exciting WORLD of MOLD

CLOUD made w science

We ran over to the table.

There was no way I was letting Beatrix take the perfect spot. So I pushed. And she shoved.

Follow That Slime

There was a stinky mess on the floor. Both of our projects were completely destroyed.

Oh no! My Exciting World of Mold!

Ew! More like the Boring World of Bad Smells!

The stinky mess had gotten up and left, leaving behind a trail of slime.

So we followed it.

Just then, we heard singing out in the hall.

Today is the day of the Science Fair,
You can feel the excitement in the air.
And on my face there is a grin,
Because this year I just might win!

Listen! The slime is singing! That cloud was my best magic EVER!!

The singing slime sounds a lot like Eddie . . .

23

Sure enough, it __was__ Eddie. He had also come to school early to set up his science project.

Eddie kept sneezing as he set his project down. Then we told him about what had happened. And we showed him the smelly trail of slime.

Together, we followed the slimy trail out into the hall. We turned a corner and saw . . . IT.

The Blob!

A super-smelly moldy blob was oozing along. And it was swallowing up everything in its path!

I looked out the window. Students were starting to arrive for the fair! We needed to trap the blob before anyone else saw it.

Eddie grabbed a tennis racket. I grabbed a volleyball net. And Beatrix took out her wand.

We set off to trap the blob.

5
Bigger and Smellier

First, we followed the trail of slime to the music room.

The smelly blob was eating up the string section!

Eddie and Beatrix helped me throw
the volleyball net up over the blob.

But the blob just oozed right through the net! It quickly made its escape back into the hallway, taking the net and half the music room with it!

Next, we followed the trail of slime to the library.

The smelly blob was eating up the books.

We held up the tennis rackets. Then we smashed, smushed, and squashed the blob to bits.

This stinky, smelly blob is done for!

No one messes with library books!

We looked around the room.

Beatrix put her hands on her hips and made a sour face.

Good job, Olly. Now the blob is <u>everywhere</u>, including all over us!

At least it's not a <u>giant</u> blob anymore. These bits can't do any damage.

A.A.ACHOO!

I don't know about that . . .

38

I heard a squish. Followed by a squash. All of the blobby bits were moving!

Then the bigger, smellier, moldy blob left the library.

We chased after the trail of slime—all the way to the art room.

The smelly blob was eating up the crayons.

But Beatrix was already casting a magic spell.

Just then—at the exact same time as Beatrix waved her wand—Eddie sneezed a GIANT sneeze.

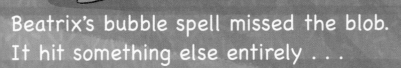

Beatrix's bubble spell missed the blob.
It hit something else entirely . . .

It hit Houston!

Not only was Houston trapped inside the bubble, but the bubble sat right in the path of the blob!

The blob moved quickly. It gulped up Houston—bubble and all!

NOOOO!!!!!!

There Goes My Pig

Beatrix was really upset. If there is one thing she really cares about, it's that talking pig.

Eddie, you ruined everything!! Why did you sneeze?!

Maybe I'm coming down with a cold ...

Hang on ... Did you say <u>cold</u>?

That's when it hit me: I knew how to stop the blob.

COLD! We make the blob cold!

You mean we make the blob sneeze?!

But it doesn't have a nose!

No, not sneeze. FREEZE!

49

We followed the slime trail yet again. This time, the smelly blob was in the cafeteria, eating up the spoons. It was waiting for us.

←KITCHEN

gobble

A-A-ACHOO!

Oh, hey, I just remembered—I'm allergic to mold.

gobble

gobble

A Little Magic, A Little Science

We were cornered!

Beatrix! Say the spell now!

Beatrix waved her wand
at the blob.

Beatrix's magic spell worked! The super-smelly moldy blob froze into a solid block of ice.

We had stopped the blob by freezing it. But now all of the stuff inside the blob was <u>really</u> trapped.

Beatrix started whacking at the ice with her wand.

Housty-Wousty!

The block of ice was not breaking.
Houston was still trapped inside.

Suddenly, the block of ice cracked into a million tiny icy bits—freeing everything inside! Frozen books, tennis rackets, violins, crayons, and Houston all crashed to the floor.

Just then, we heard noises coming from the kitchen.

And the Winner Is . . .

Eddie and I scrambled to pick up the icy bits of blob.

We sprinted back and forth to the walk-in freezer.

Finally, we had cleaned up all of the icy bits. But there was still a big pile of damp school supplies.

The loud speaker crackled on.

Attention, students! Please come to the gym. We will announce the winner of this year's Science Fair in ten minutes.

Beatrix was a speedy flyer. She quickly returned all of the books, tennis rackets, crayons, violins, chairs, and ukuleles. She even returned a sock to the Lost-and-Found.

We rushed to the gym.

Everyone headed to the cafeteria for lunch.

So, even though our projects came alive and nearly swallowed the whole school, the Science Fair turned out pretty great.

That is, until dessert was served.

The next day, some students called out sick with a stomachache. The lunch ladies never did figure out where all those green Jell-O molds came from . . .

Amy Marie Stadelmann

Amy did not grow up with a sister who was a witch, or with a talking pig. But she did grow up with a <u>very</u> active imagination! She often imagined that she had magical powers and could talk to animals. Like Olive, Amy once dreamed of winning her school Science Fair. And, like Beatrix, she often chooses cupcakes for dessert! Amy lives in Brooklyn, New York, with a non-talking dog. Olive & Beatrix is her first children's book series.

Olive & Beatrix

Questions and Activities!

Look at the pictures on pages 4 and 5. How do Olive and Beatrix take a cookie from the jar in different ways?

How does Beatrix use magic and how does Olive use science to solve the blob problem? Provide examples.

What causes the blob to form?

Why don't Olive, Beatrix, and Eddie want to eat their original desserts?

Reread Eddie's songs on pages 10 and 23. Pick out the rhyming words. Think of two new pairs of words that rhyme. Then write a song!